You can count on

Fergie

NOVALIS

TWENTY-THIRD PUBLICATIONS
A Division of Bayard   MYSTIC, CT 06355

© 2002 Novalis, Saint Paul University, Ottawa, Canada

Cover design and layout: Caroline Gagnon

The illustrations were done using mixed technique: crayons, gouache and ink.

Business Office:
Novalis
49 Front Street East, 2nd Floor
Toronto, Ontario, Canada
M5E 1B3

Phone: 1-800-387-7164 or (416) 363-3303
Fax: 1-800-204-4140 or (416) 363-9409
E-mail: cservice@novalis.ca

Published in the United States by
Twenty-Third Publications
A Division of Bayard
185 Willow Street
P.O. Box 180
Mystic, CT 06355
(860) 536-2611
(800) 321-0411
www.twentythirdpublications.com

National Library of Canada Cataloguing in Publication Data
Cocks, Nancy, 1954–
     You can count on Fergie

(The new adventures of Fergie the frog)
ISBN 2-89507-272-8

Marton, Jirina II. Title. III. Series: Cocks, Nancy, 1954– .
New adventures of Fergie the frog.

PS8555.O2854Y69 2002   jC813'.54   C2002-900891-3
PZ7

U.S. ISBN: 1-58595-226-5

Printed in Canada.

We acknowledge the financial support of the Government of Canada through the Book Publishing Industry Development Program (BPIDP) for our publishing activities.

10 9 8 7 6 5 4 3 2 1   10 09 08 07 06 05 04 03 02

To my sister, Jane
—N.C.

To Leonard
—J.M.

Fergie the Frog hopped home from school one day. "Hey, Mom!" he called. "There's a new kid in my class at school. Do you think I could bring her home for supper sometime?"

"Who's your new girlfriend, Fergie?" his mother asked as she stirred the spider legs into the stew.

"Mo-o-om, Tanya Turtle is *not* my girlfriend. But she is the greatest in math! She said she would help me with my times tables. So I thought maybe you could make flyloaf and mashed mushrooms with gravy one day soon. Flyloaf is Tanya's favourite!"

"I see," said Mother Frog. "I guess when you're seven, math is more important than romance. Flyloaf it is! How about Friday?"

"Mo-o-om! I am *not* in love with Tanya Turtle. I just like her. OK?" Fergie grinned.

On Friday after school, Tanya and Fergie set off for the swamp.

"Thanks for inviting me for supper," said Tanya. "It's hard making friends at this school. Lots of frogs tease me because I'm a turtle and I can't hop very well. Actually, I can't hop at all!"

"That's OK, Tanya. You can do math all right. And that's what counts," said Fergie. "Heh, heh, heh!"

Tanya giggled. "Good one, Fergie!"

All of a sudden, three big frogs jumped out of the bushes and blocked their path. "Hey, Fergie, you got a new girlfriend?" one of them said in a mean voice.

"Guess she couldn't move fast enough to get away from you," another croaked.

"C'mon, you guys," said Fergie. "Leave us alone."

"Or did you sweep her off her feet?" the third frog teased. He hopped right over Tanya. "Nah, couldn't be. It would take more than a pint-sized tadpole like Fergie to get this tub of a turtle off her feet. Let's give her a hand!"

The three big bully frogs flipped Tanya the Turtle onto her back. Tanya pulled her legs and her head inside her shell and lay in the middle of the path.

"Help me, Fergie. I can't turn myself over," Tanya cried from inside her shell.

Fergie hopped to Tanya's side. "Hey, leave her alone," he said to the bullies. "She wasn't hurting you."

"Maybe we should stick you in there with her," said one of the big frogs. He grabbed a stick and hopped toward Fergie. "Come here, you little tad-poke!"

Fergie took off, hopping as fast as he could.

One of the bullies shouted, "Look at the little green flea hop! What about your girlfriend, Fergie?"

When Fergie got home, Mother Frog was just putting the flyloaf in the oven. "Where's your friend?" she asked.

"Quick, Mom! Quick, Freddie! We have to go save Tanya from a gang of big bully frogs. Follow me!" Fergie called.

When the three of them reached Tanya the Turtle, the bullies were gone.

"Tanya, it's OK. It's me, Fergie, with my mom and my brother, Freddie. We'll flip you right side up!" Then the three frogs gently flipped Tanya over.

When Tanya was back on her feet again, she said, "Thanks for coming back, Fergie. When I heard you hopping away, I thought you were gone for good. You saved me from turning into turtle soup!"

Fergie blushed a little. "Well, Tanya," he said, "I may not be very good at math, but you can always count on me!"

"Good one, Fergie," Tanya giggled.

Friends are people we can count on – to help us with little problems like math, or to be there when we're in big trouble. Jesus calls us his friends. We can count on him to be with us when we're in trouble, and his love can help us to be good friends for other people to count on.

Jesus, I am glad to be your friend. Be there with me when I have problems big or small. Help me remember that I can count on your love to make things better. Amen.